$4.79

E
c.1

Zemach, Harve
        A penny a look

APR 19   WS12789
NOV 1   WS 7500
MAR 31   WS
MAY 13   WS14272
MAY 13   WS14272

E
c.1

Zemach, Harve
        A penny a look; an old story retold
by Harve Zemach. Pictures by Margot
Zemach.   Farrar [c1971]
        [40] p.   illus.

4.79

PICTURES BY MARGOT ZEMACH

A PENNY A LOOK

AN OLD STORY RETOLD BY

HARVE ZEMACH

FARRAR · STRAUS · GIROUX · NEW YORK

This book is dedicated to our children

Rachel, Heidi, Kaethe, Rebecca

Once there were two brothers. Everybody called the older one a red-headed rascal. "No doubt about it," people said, "he's got what it takes. Some day he'll be rich!"

/

The other brother was different. People called him a lazy good-for-nothing, because he hated to work. "Don't pay any attention to that one," they said. "He'll never amount to much. He'll never get anywhere. He's a lazy good-for-nothing."

The red-headed rascal had lots of ideas. One day he said to his brother: "Listen! I just found a map that shows the way to a place where some one-eyed people live. All we have to do is go there and capture a one-eyed man, bring him back home, put him in a cage in the marketplace, and charge a penny a look. We'll make millions!"

"Is that so?" said the lazy good-for-nothing. "Well, you go ahead and catch a one-eyed man, and when you get back maybe I'll help you collect the pennies."

"Oh, no! You have to come with me," said the red-headed rascal, who thought he might need help to catch a one-eyed man. "Just to keep me company on the trip," he said.

The lazy good-for-nothing didn't want to, but the red-headed rascal finally persuaded him to go along, as a favor for a brother. They started out the next day, taking with them only the map and a rope for tying up the one-eyed man when he was captured.

They had to go a long way. They had to drive five hundred miles in an automobile; and while they were driving, the lazy good-for-nothing said: "By the way, what will we give him to eat?"

"Who?" said the red-headed rascal.

"The one-eyed man . . . when we have him back home in the cage?"

"Oh, him. Don't worry," said the red-headed rascal. "Scraps and crumbs. We won't let him starve. I've got it all figured out."

Then they had to wade across a stream, and while they were wading, the lazy good-for-nothing said: "By the way, is he going to have to stay in that cage *all* the time?"

"Who?" said the red-headed rascal.

"The one-eyed man."

"Oh, him. Of course he is. You don't think we'd give him a chance to try any tricks, after going to all this trouble to capture him! Now stop worrying and leave everything to me."

9

Then they had to climb over some fences. While they were climbing, the lazy good-for-nothing said: "By the way, he isn't going to like it very much, is he?"

"Who?" said the red-headed rascal.

"The one-eyed man. He isn't going to like it with all those people staring at him all the time, is he?"

"Oh, him. That's all right. Like it or not, he won't be able to do anything about it. So no need to worry."

Then they had to fly over a desert in a balloon. While they were flying, the lazy good-for-nothing said: "You know, I can't help feeling that maybe it's not right."

"What?" said the red-headed rascal.

"Maybe it's not right to do this to a poor, helpless one-eyed man."

"Don't be silly," said the red-headed rascal. "Forget about him. Think of all the pennies."

Finally, they arrived. "This is the place!" cried the red-headed rascal. "Now let's catch the first one we find."

They looked around and all they could see was a pile of rocks. Suddenly, from behind the rocks, there appeared . . .

. . . a one-eyed man.
The brothers ran to catch him.

But just then a second one-eyed man appeared.

16

Then a whole bunch of one-eyed men came
rushing up.

They caught the red-headed rascal and the lazy
good-for-nothing and carried them to *their* town.

And they put the red-headed rascal in a cage in the middle of the marketplace and charged everybody a penny a look to see a two-eyed man with red hair!

They didn't pay much attention to the lazy good-for-nothing, because they could see he would never amount to much. They knew he would never get anywhere. So they let him collect the pennies. He didn't mind.

Printed by Pearl Pressman Liberty, Philadelphia
Bound by Montauk Book Manufacturing Company, Harrison, New Jersey
Typography by Atha Tehon